Avon Lake Public Library
32649 Electric Blvd.
Avon Lake, Ohio 44012

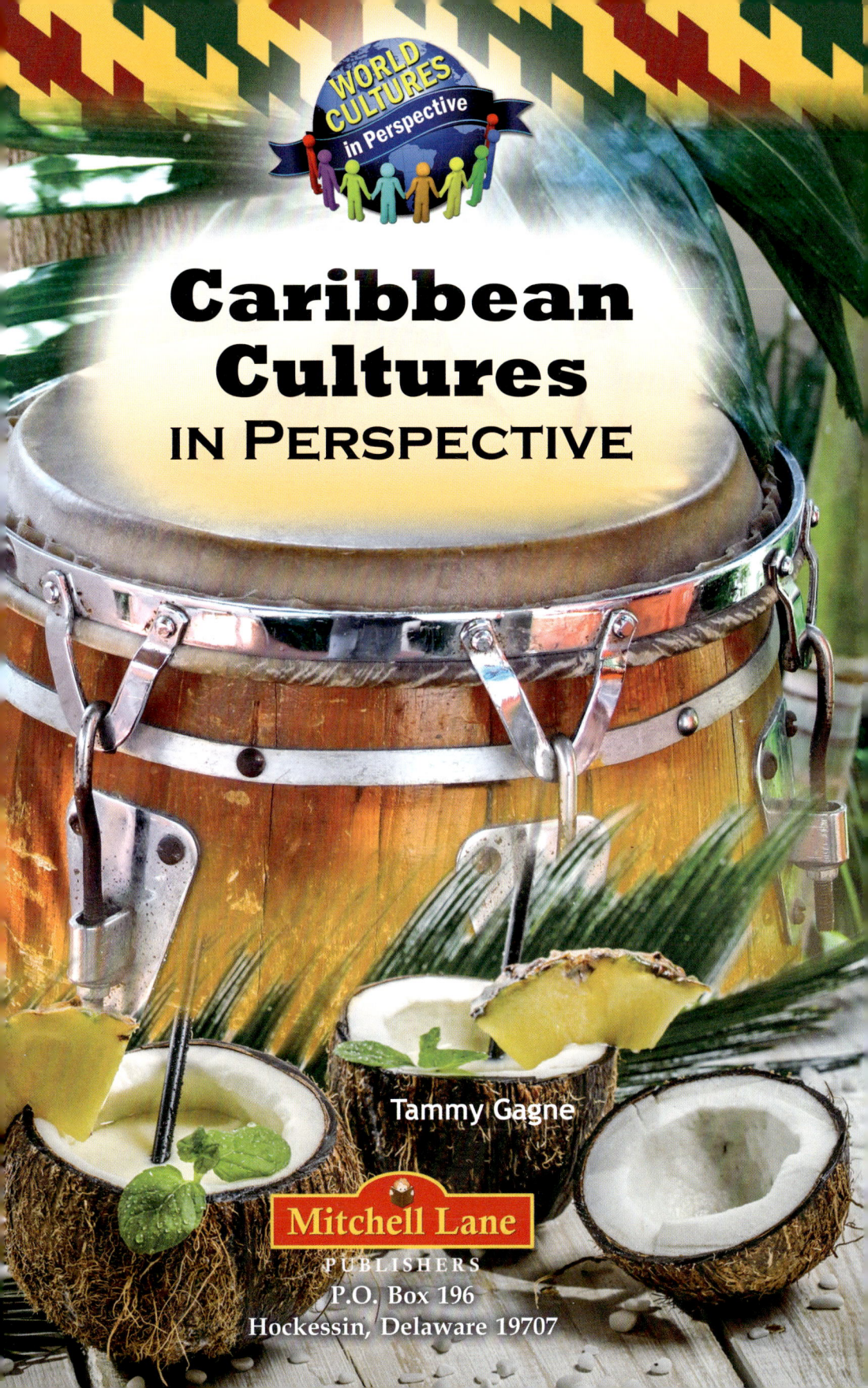

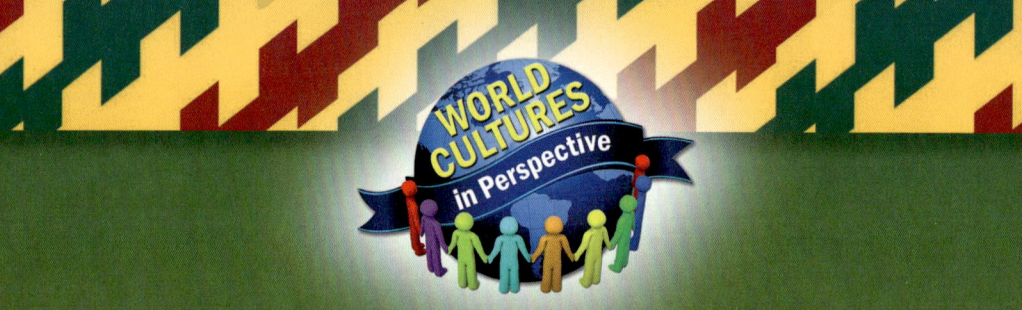

Brazilian Cultures IN PERSPECTIVE

Caribbean Cultures IN PERSPECTIVE

East Asian Cultures IN PERSPECTIVE

Islamic Culture IN PERSPECTIVE

Israeli Culture IN PERSPECTIVE

Louisiana Cajun & Creole Cultures IN PERSPECTIVE

Native Alaskan Cultures IN PERSPECTIVE

North African Cultures IN PERSPECTIVE

Polynesian Cultures IN PERSPECTIVE

Southeast Asian Cultures IN PERSPECTIVE

Copyright © 2015 by Mitchell Lane Publishers, Inc. All rights reserved. No part of this book may be reproduced without written permission from the publisher. Printed and bound in the United States of America.

Printing   1   2   3   4   5   6   7   8   9

Library of Congress Cataloging-in-Publication Data
Gagne, Tammy.
 Caribbean cultures in perspective / by Tammy Gagne.
    pages cm. — (World cultures in perspective)
 Includes bibliographical references and index.
 ISBN 978-1-61228-559-7 (library bound)
 1. Caribbean Area--Juvenile literature. I. Title.
 F2161.5.G34 2014
 972.9—dc23
                                        2014009361

eBook ISBN: 9781612285986

PUBLISHER'S NOTE: This story is based on the author's extensive research, which she believes to be accurate. Documentation of this research is on pages 59–61.
    The Internet sites referenced herein were active as of the publication date. Due to the fleeting nature of some web sites, we cannot guarantee they will all be active when you are reading this book.

PBP

CONTENTS

Introduction 6
Chapter 1: BARBADOS 8
   Music of the Sun 14
Chapter 2: JAMAICA 16
   Serious Competitors 20
Chapter 3: TRINIDAD AND TOBAGO 22
   Nicki Minaj 28
Chapter 4: PUERTO RICO AND THE
US VIRGIN ISLANDS 30
   The 51st State? 35
Chapter 5: CUBA 36
   An American Icon in Cuba 41
Chapter 6: HAITI 42
   Holding on to Her Heritage 47
Chapter 7: THE BAHAMAS 48
   Forty Years and Counting 54
Experiencing Caribbean Culture in the United States 55
Map of the Caribbean 56
Chapter Notes 57
Further Reading 59
   Books 59
   On the Internet 59
   Works Consulted 59
Glossary 62
Index 63

Introduction

To many people around the world, the Caribbean is a glorious vacation destination. With over 7,000 islands, this tropical region between North and South America draws legions of visitors each year. Its turquoise waters, white-sand beaches, and warm climate make the Caribbean a magical spot.

The Caribbean is named for the Carib Indians, a fierce people whom Christopher Columbus and other early explorers encountered during their

voyages of discovery. Columbus was searching for a western route to India, so he gave the name of Indians to the Caribs and other peoples who had lived there for centuries. Later the region would be called the West Indies to differentiate it from the East Indies, the name given to the vast area of South and Southeast Asia that Columbus had hoped to reach.

Many island economies depend on money from visitors. But to the people who call these islands home, the area is much more than pretty photos in a brochure. The islands share a great deal of history and culture. Each island also has its own unique past and customs.

Chapter One
Barbados

While early Spanish and Portuguese explorers visited Barbados, in 1627 the British became the first Europeans to settle there. Soon thereafter wealthy Englishmen were given land on the island to establish plantations. The fertile soil was ideal for growing cotton, sugar cane, and tobacco.

At first, the landowners relied on indentured servants to work the land. These impoverished white people agreed to work for five to seven years in exchange for their voyage from Europe to the Caribbean. Soon it became clear that there weren't enough indentured servants. The landowners began importing African slaves. Slavery was finally abolished in 1834, enabling the newly freed slaves to attend school and get better jobs. Barbados became independent in 1966. But it remains closely linked with Great Britain, as part of the Commonwealth of Nations. Many wealthy British citizens own homes on the island, which is known for combining the luxuries of Europe with the balmy climate of the Caribbean and a relaxed pace of life.

James Burdess moved to Barbados 13 years ago. "The beaches, the sea breezes, the culture and the people are all fantastic," he said, "but it is the things you don't see that make me want to live here—the schools, the hospitals and the sport. Here it's a return to old-school values—the crime rate is negligible, people still get dressed up to go out in the evenings and the golf courses are incredible. . . . You can do everything you do in England, but it's warm."[1]

Wealthy British make up a small percentage of the population. Descendants of the African slaves who once labored on the plantations account for 93 percent of the inhabitants of Barbados. For this reason African culture is a main part of the island's unique mix of art, music, and food.

Bridgetown, Barbados, was once named Indian Bridge, after a primitive bridge that stretched over the Careenage River.

Chapter One

This unique mix attracts visitors who flock to the island. As British journalist John Wilmott wrote, though, the natives make the island so special. "Show an interest in a Barbadian's cooking, music, handiwork, sporting ability or gardening skill and he or she will delight in explaining their craft. The wide grins encountered at every turn are often cited as a reason why many visitors keep returning to Barbados."[2]

Visitors can also tour mansions that once belonged to the island's plantation owners and are now filled with antiques. These artifacts show locals and tourists what life was like. Many families who visit Barbados enjoy Arlington House, an interactive heritage museum. The island also includes beautiful churches.

Those interested in livelier aspects of Barbadian culture can take part in a variety of festivals, featuring upbeat music and lots of food. The largest is the Crop Over Festival in July and August, which celebrates the year's sugar cane harvest. Many people also

Arlington House, built in 1750.

Barbados

The Crop Over Festival, which celebrates the year's sugar cane harvest, began in 1780.

take part in the Oistins Fish Festival, which celebrates the island's fishing industry and features live reggae music, dancing, and fried fish.

Interestingly, the United States has had a significant effect on Barbados, which has adopted many American traditions. These influences can be found in fashion, food, and music. And the Barbados dollar is linked to the US dollar.

American influence doesn't extend to baseball, however. Journalist Mark Eklid explained that "Cricket is just one of the British traits that remain in Barbados." Calling the sport "the greatest game of all," he added that the British "allowed [the Barbadians] to humiliate us at our own game."[3]

Chapter One

Cricket is just one of many sports that visitors can enjoy in Barbados. As Senator Irene Sandiford-Garner pointed out, "Barbados has evolved as an outstanding sports destination. In fact, we have over 60 sports disciplines on the island and we come from a long line of excellence in sports with the likes of the Right Excellent Sir Garfield Sobers, the greatest cricketer the world has ever seen; two-time Mr. Universe body building champion, Earl Maynard; bronze medalist at the Sydney Olympics, Obadele Thompson; 110 meters hurdles champion in the 2009 World Championship, Ryan Brathwaite; and champion jockey in Canada, Patrick Husbands."[4]

Barbados offers visitors a wide variety of department stores, restaurants, and hotels—especially in Bridgetown, the island's capital, where about 40 percent of Barbadians live. It has been called "one of the most sophisticated ports in the Caribbean."[5]

Lendl Simmons bats during a cricket match between England and the West Indies in 2014. Barbados won this three-series match 2 to 1.

Barbadian-born jockey Patrick Husbands has more than 2,700 wins to his credit.

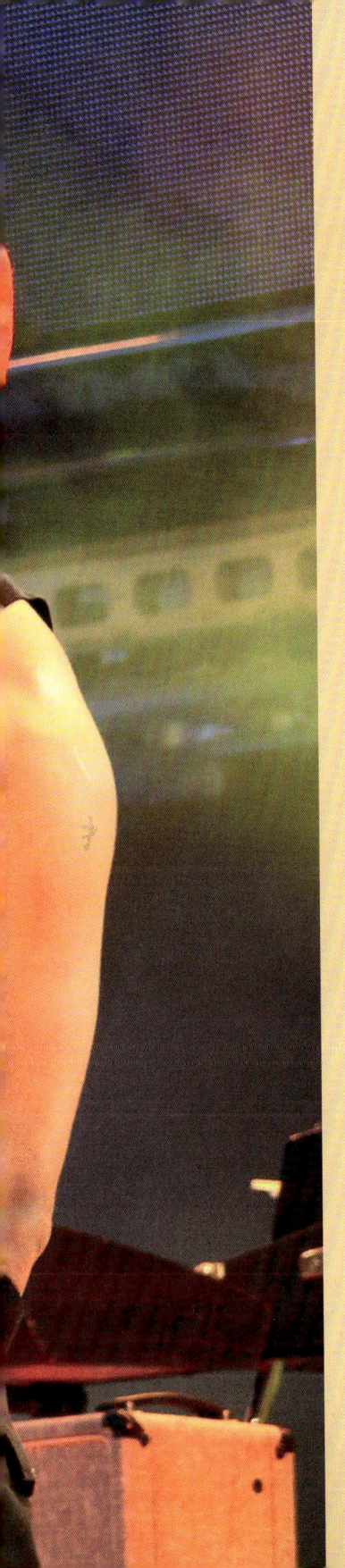

Music of the Sun

Robyn Rihanna Fenty was born in St. Michael Parish, Barbados, in 1988. Now known simply as Rihanna, she is among the most successful R&B singers in the world. Although she left Barbados at 15 to pursue her music career, she returns home whenever she can.

Def Jam Records president Shaun "Jay-Z" Carter remembers when he first heard Rihanna sing. "I signed her in one day. It took me two minutes to see she was a star."[6] Signing the artist proved to be a smart move. By the end of 2013, Rihanna had sold $10 million in albums in the United States alone.

Some people criticize her for her daring fashion choices. She is known for wearing revealing outfits both on and off stage. She is unapologetic. "Going back to carnival in Barbados this year I really noticed it is a cultural thing, it is the way we move," she explained. "We are half naked and having a good time."[7]

Rihanna has never forgotten her roots in Barbados. She has returned to the island several times to give concerts. Several promotional videos depict her doing many of the things that make her island so attractive to tourists. And in 2012, she donated nearly $2 million to the Queen Elizabeth Hospital to honor her grandmother, who had died earlier that year.

Born in Barbados, Rihanna has risen to international fame in recent years. She performs here at the Italian TV festival in Trieste, Italy.

Chapter Two
Jamaica

Like many Caribbean islands, Jamaica was once a British colony. It became independent in 1962. By then it had become a popular vacation spot for the rich and famous. President John F. Kennedy and his wife, Jackie, honeymooned on the island. Many actors and writers even bought second homes on the island. Ian Fleming wrote 14 James Bond novels at his Goldeneye villa in Oracabessa Bay. Today Jamaica is affordable for both wealthy and middle-class travelers who enjoy sun, relaxation, and pampering on an island especially noted for its reggae music, food, and laid-back atmosphere. Jamaica's service industry is regarded as among the best in the world.

The locals see Jamaica as a symbol of the Caribbean. Real estate agent Nicola Delapenha explained, "Jamaica is unique because we have so much indigenous culture. I'm always amused when I travel elsewhere in the Caribbean, and any time you see live music, the first song is always [Jamaican singer and songwriter] Bob Marley or another of our singers. Everyone knows [native

Jamaican] jerk chicken around the world. We are also very diverse for an island."[1]

Some families have lived on the island for generations. Others settled in Jamaica from different parts of the world. Despite their different backgrounds, the population is amazingly interconnected. Jamaica's motto is "Out of many, one people." Jamaicans find unity in simply being Jamaican.

More than 1,700 miles from Jamaica, the Canadian city of Toronto is home to many people with ties to Jamaica. *Toronto Star* journalist Ashante Infantry was born in Canada. But she spent the first nine years of her life in the island's capital of Kingston with her grandmother. Infantry thinks her Jamaican roots helped her deal with being black in a mostly white country. "Growing up seeing people like me populating every role, I was later secure in knowing that the deficiency of North Americans still marking the first black this or that in the 20th century was not mine,"[2] she wrote.

Ocho Rios is a major port of call in Jamaica.

Chapter Two

Toronto Star baseball columnist Richard Griffin was also born in Jamaica. "The early years in Jamaica had a lasting impact on my life," he recalled. "I had sporting heroes, boxer Bunny Grant, cricketers Garfield Sobers and Wesley Hall. So Jamaican athletes like [Olympic sprint champion] Usain Bolt resonate with me. . . . My Twitter homepage has a background of the Jamaican flag, and when I took my children there for a vacation it was a warm feeling of going home."[3]

Chantaie Allick is a *Toronto Star* intern. Like Infantry, she was born in Canada. But her mother was born in Jamaica. "I'm so proud of my mother and grandmother and how hard they've

Jarvan Gallimore of Jamaica during 400m hurdles event of the 20th World Junior Athletics Championships at the Olympic Stadium on July 11, 2012 in Barcelona, Spain.

worked to establish themselves here after leaving Jamaica for better opportunities. They embody the Jamaican ethic of stoic hard work. . . . I'm glad for the Jamaican part of my identity and hope my kids will have the same sense of pride in their heritage that I have."[4]

Allick is grateful to her family for keeping Jamaican cuisine part of their lives. "I love ackee and salt fish—my family eats it every Christmas morning. . . . I've visited Jamaica, and the palm trees, jelly coconuts, crayfish, machetes, Beacon Hill and rivers are all in my bones and blood."[5]

Food is indeed a large part of Jamaican culture. Among the most popular indigenous dishes are Jamaican patties. These pastries look like yellow turnovers. But they are savory instead of sweet. The golden color comes from an egg mixture made with turmeric, a popular Caribbean spice. Another popular treat is fried plantains. And locals rave about oxtail soup.

Jamaica's music is as unique as its food. No artist is as much a symbol of the island's music culture as Bob Marley. Although he died in 1981, his reggae songs can still be heard all over the island. Many other reggae artists—including Marley's son Ziggy—have put their own touches on the style. Jamaican music includes many other styles. Dancehall, dub, mento, ska, and folk music are all part of Jamaican—and Caribbean—culture.

Jamaican patties

Serious Competitors

Despite living in a tropical climate, a group of Jamaican men decided to compete in bobsledding at the 1988 Winter Olympics. Jamaica had never had a bobsled team. In fact the nation had few winter competitors. The men quickly became the object of jokes. After all, how could anyone from the Caribbean perform sports involving snow and ice? Where would they even train?

Captain Dudley Stokes was a pilot in the Jamaican Defence Force. Until he joined the team, he didn't even understand how bobsleds worked. "What fired up my imagination was the discovery that a bobsled had to be driven. I thought it was just like a rollercoaster ride, even when I watched it on TV. Then I discovered that if you messed it up you could be in real trouble."[6]

Businessman George Fitch formed the team. He had watched Jamaican pushcart races and saw similarities between the two sports. He asked US coach Howard Siler to help him take the men to the Calgary Olympics. "We're serious athletes," Stokes insisted. "We came here to be competitive. There are no jokers on this team."[7]

The Jamaicans showed their critics just how serious they were. The team fulfilled its goal of making it to the Calgary games, an accomplishment only a select group of people throughout the world can claim. The 1993 Disney movie *Cool Runnings* is based on the team's story.

Dudley Stokes and his three teammates were the first Jamaican competitors in Olympic bobsledding at the 1988 Calgary Games. Here they push off at the beginning of their second run.

Chapter Three
Trinidad and Tobago

Trinidad and the nearby island of Tobago used to be separate. But they united in 1889, forming a single colony under British control. The colony gained independence from Great Britain in 1962 and became known as the Republic of Trinidad and Tobago. Trinidad is the larger and more populous of the two, with an area of 1,833 square miles (4,478 sq km) and a population of about 1,300,000. Tobago's area is 116 square miles (300 sq km), and about 60,000 people live there.

Some call the nation a melting pot. This means that the various cultures have blended together over the years. Today people use the slang term "Trinbagonian" to describe the joint culture of the islands. But each island also has its own history and traditions.

Great Britain captured Trinidad in 1797 from the Spanish. The British wanted the island for its fertile soil and shipped African slaves across the Atlantic Ocean to work the sugar plantations. Eventually, slavery was abolished. But the British soon found another source of labor. They brought indentured servants from China, India, and the Middle East. Some people feel the variety of influences gives the nation the most diverse culture in the Caribbean.

Trinidad native Tara Kraft explained to the *Tribune Business News*, "In Trinidad, we celebrate Arrival Day, because the Indians who went to Trinidad, the British fooled them, told them they were going there on a contract, but they never got to go back. The Africans, they have their own emancipation day, and the Chinese have their own celebrations. It is a land made up of all different ethnics, so they give everyone their own holiday. . . . I grew up in the country, but I was the only Indian kid where we were living.

Flag-raising ceremonies in August 1962 at the Red House, the seat of Parliament, mark the independence of Trinidad and Tobago from the British Empire.

Chapter Three

My grandpa decided we needed to move to the central, where all the Indians lived, so I could learn about my culture."[1]

A deep respect between the various cultures exists in Trinidad. The people value their own traditions without looking down on others. Kraft, who now lives in Worthington, Minnesota, sees this as a big difference between the United States and her home country. "Everybody has respect for everyone else [in Trinidad]," she pointed out. "I think there is prejudice [in the US] still. There, you could be black, white, and people don't notice it. We are proud of being our culture, and we feel that love with everybody. . . . Trinidad is something like Worthington, with all the different ethnic groups. I think it's why I adjust so well here. When I go to Wal-Mart, I feel like I'm in Trinidad."[2]

One holiday that everyone in Trinidad celebrates is Carnival. Even people who aren't from Trinidad travel there for this annual festival. It takes place on the Monday and Tuesday before Ash Wednesday. The celebration includes large parades, music, dancing, and wildly colorful costumes.

Another significant difference between Trinidad and the US involves education. In Trinidad, a college education is free to all citizens. Kraft took advantage of this opportunity when she lived on the island. She studied manufacturing and opened her own company after graduating. "I had my own business, Blue J's Garments. We made kids clothes, nightgowns, school uniforms, Carnival costumes. I had 17 girls working for me,"[3] she said.

Although Kraft moved the US when she got married, she still feels a strong connection to the island. When her mother passed away, she inherited her childhood home. She hopes to turn it into a vacation home for her own family.

Tobago has a tumultuous history. The island changed rulers 33 times before the British finally assumed control in 1814. Its economy is tightly connected with Trinidad.

Both islands are seeking to develop themselves as tourist destinations, as they are among the least-visited of the major Caribbean islands.

Trinidad and Tobago features parades, filled with colorfully costumed masqueraders, that are popular with tourists.

Chapter Three

The music of Trinidad and Tobago could be a source of increased tourism. Jenny Morgan of Oregon's Linfield College and a group of her classmates spent an entire month there as part of a course called Music Cultures of the World: Trinidad and Tobago.

The students visited with Trinidadian musicians. They listened to Calypso singers perform live and even visited Carnival mask-maker studios. The goal was to educate the young people about diverse musical genres. "It was incredible," Morgan said. "They have such a vibrant culture but very different from the States. We met so many wonderful musicians, and the people there were very friendly."[4]

Morgan's visit was typical for students interested in learning about Trinidad's culture. In 2013, the nation awarded 30 university scholarships to young people from Nigeria. These students would study costume making as well as carnival management during their stay.

Dr. Lincoln Douglas is Trinidad and Tobago's Minister of Arts and Multiculturalism. He saw the program as something that would benefit both the students and his own nation. "This [is] a great opportunity for Nigeria and Trinidad and Tobago," he said. "We want to share our skills in the area of street carnival and music which we have been doing for 17 years. So, this is a platform to bring people together to know each other."[5]

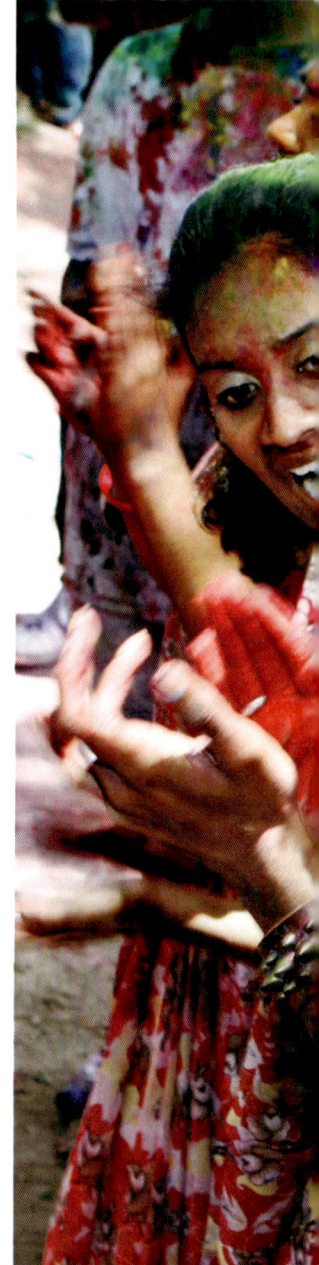

Trinidad and Tobago

This Phagwa celebration at Tunapuna Hindu School on Trinidad is part of a spring festival also known as the festival of colors or festival of love.

Nicki Minaj

One of Trinidad's best-known musicians is rap singer Nicki Minaj. She was born in St. James, Port of Spain, Trinidad in 1982. Her mother and father moved to New York City when the little girl was three. Nicki lived with her grandmother and other members of her extended family in a small home for two years, then went to New York to be with her parents. She grew up in a neighborhood called Jamaica, Queens, made up largely of people of Caribbean descent.

Today Minaj is one of the most unique artists in music. Many even go as far as labeling her strange. "I don't mind being called a weirdo," she has insisted. "There are a lot of people in hip-hop who are probably never going to get what I do. But, by just being myself, I end up touching a lot more people who might never have paid much attention to a female rapper."[6]

Minaj made a name for herself for her racy look and outspoken personality as much as for her music. She sees herself as a role model regardless. "I made a conscious decision to try to tone down the sexiness. I want people—especially young girls—to know that in life, nothing is going to be based on sex appeal. You've got to have something else to go with that."[7]

Nicki Minaj filmed parts of her 2012 video "Pound the Alarm" in her native city of Port of Spain, seen here.

In 2013, Nicki Minaj served as a judge on the television singing competition *American Idol*.

Chapter Four
Puerto Rico and the US Virgin Islands

The United States has two Caribbean territories: Puerto Rico and the US Virgin Islands. Citizens in both territories are US citizens. Very few pay federal income tax. While they can vote in local elections, they cannot vote for the US president.

Christopher Columbus arrived in Puerto Rico in November 1493, during his second voyage, and claimed it for Spain. Like many Caribbean islands, it became known for its abundant crops. Coffee, sugar cane, and tobacco all flourished in Puerto Rico. And also like many other islands, African slaves were brought in to work those crops.

Because of the money its crops produced, Puerto Rico attracted the attention of many other countries. England, France, and the Netherlands all tried to take the island by force. But none was successful. The Spaniards built numerous forts on the island to help protect it. Puerto Rico remained under their rule until the Spanish-American War in 1898, when the island became US property.

Due to its long history with Spain, Puerto Rico remains rich in Spanish culture. Both English and Spanish are official languages. It has also adopted some of the customs from African slaves who were brought to the island.

Author Ronald Flores notes that Puerto Rico shares many qualities with other Caribbean islands. "All the islands share a similar marvelous natural setting, beaches and weather; you might say that if you've seen one picture-perfect tropical beach, you've

Luquillo Beach, Puerto Rico

Chapter Four

seen them all," he said. "But that's not all: Puerto Rico has singular attractions: Old San Juan [the island's oldest settlement] is at the top of my list. Every time I walk in the Old City I get goose bumps—I lived there for three years and never got over the feeling that I was somewhere special, the center of a unique universe."[1]

Asked what makes Puerto Rico different, Flores says the people and the food are at the top of the list. The island calls itself the "Culinary Capital of the Caribbean." Flores insists this is an apt nickname. "Nowhere else in the region can you find such a huge variety of high-quality restaurants and world-class chefs," he explained. "The most important distinction is the character of the people. I have traveled extensively and each place I go promotes the hospitality of its people. People are people. Some are naturally friendly and some are not. Latinos tend to be friendlier than most; Puerto Ricans tend to be the friendliest."[2]

Adal Maldonado has been an artist for more than four decades, and spent much of that time expressing what it means to be Puerto Rican. "We are multilayered because so many different cultures and races came through Puerto Rico with the slave trade. We became a sort of fusion of all those experiences and ideas. I was raised to feel that I had many different dimensions that I could choose from,"[3] he said.

He chose to explore Puerto Rican culture through pictures. His book *Portraits of the Puerto Rican Experience* includes photographs and interviews of 100 Puerto Ricans who have risen to the top of their fields. Some were artists like Maldonado, others were scientists, still others worked in community service. His book was so effective that the New York City school system began using it as part of its social studies classes.

Maldonado's work suggests that Puerto Rico is a symbol of the future. "Eventually, everyone will be a hybrid of something," he asserted. "Whether it's Asian or Latino, we're all going to look alike."[4]

The US Virgin Islands are part of the larger Virgin Islands archipelago, which consists of seven larger islands and hundreds of smaller ones. Columbus discovered them during the same

Puerto Rico and the US Virgin Islands

voyage as his discovery of Puerto Rico. Today they are divided between Great Britain and the United States, which purchased its share from Denmark in 1917. The US Virgins consist primarily of three large islands—St. Croix, St. John, and St. Thomas—and tiny Water Island, which was added in 1996.

Because they are part of the United States, the islands have adopted many American customs. At the same time, they have developed their own culture. As a result, from food and fashion to music and sports, life here is both familiar and fresh to visitors.

Pates are one of the most popular food items in the islands. Made from fried dough, they can be filled with spiced meat, fish, or vegetables. Many tourists love pates so much that they

Puerto Rican day parade celebration in New York City. Puerto Rico is part of the US and residents can travel back and forth between the island and continental US.

Chapter Four

immediately want the recipe. But they are unlikely to get it. Locals do not use recipes, cooking instead from memory. Even if a recipe was written down, it would simply instruct the cook to use "a little bit" of this or that.

While the official language is English, many islanders also speak Creole, French-Patois, and Spanish. This variety of languages is a reflection of the varied origins of the people, of whom more than 75 percent are black or Afro-Caribbean.

The music heard on the islands is as varied as everything else. Traditional Caribbean music like calypso, reggae, and steel pan is played in many clubs. But blues, jazz, Latin music, and even classical performances are also common.

Steel drum player, US Virgin Islands

The 51st State?

People have been talking about granting Puerto Rico statehood for many years. Several movements for statehood dating back to 1967 went nowhere. In 2012, for the first time, there was a referendum to see what the Puerto Rican people wanted. The results were a bit confusing.

The referendum consisted of two questions. First, it asked the people if they wanted to continue to be a territory. Then it asked if they wanted to become a state or some other option. The vote on the first question was 54 percent to 46 percent in favor of a different status. With regard to the second question, while nearly 45 percent voted in favor of statehood, about one-fourth of the voters chose not to answer the question at all. That means that 61 percent of the people who did answer the question were in favor of becoming a state.

Many people think that the chances of Puerto Rico becoming a state are slim. Opponents say that statehood would require Puerto Ricans to pay billions more in federal taxes. Those in favor insist that federal benefits would increase. The island would also gain two US senators and at least one member in the House of Representatives.

Early in 2014, US Senator Martin Heinrich introduced a bill calling for a simple yes-or-no vote among Puerto Ricans with regard to the statehood issue. "My home state of New Mexico spent 66 years as a territory before gaining statehood in 1912—the longest of any state," he said. "Puerto Rico has spent nearly 116 years as an American territory. That's long enough."[5]

Even if this vote is held, it doesn't guarantee that Puerto Rico would be admitted as a state. The US Congress makes the final determination.

A voter casts his ballot in the 2012 referendum on the issue of statehood.

Chapter Five
Cuba

When most people think of the Caribbean, they think of islands such as Barbados, Jamaica, or Puerto Rico that they might want to visit someday. Few, however, are likely to include Cuba on their wish list. Even though it is less than 100 miles (160 kilometers) from Florida, Cuba has been largely off-limits to Americans since 1961 when a revolution led by Fidel Castro installed a communist government on the island. Since then exceptions have been made for members of the State Department, journalists, and a handful of business people. Today exceptions can also be made for those participating in programs such as People-to-People, a cultural exchange organization that aims to educate people all over the world by bringing them together.

Certainly, visiting Cuba is a lot different than traveling to countries with friendlier relations with the United States. But most visitors realize pretty quickly that the Cuban people are much like people in other parts of the world. And their culture is equally interesting.

Travel expert Peggy Goldman wrote of Cuba, "Time there has stood still, which is readily apparent as soon as you step off the plane. It's truly the shortest distance you'll ever travel to enter an entirely different world. But if you're open-minded and appreciate history, culture rich in art and music, resourcefulness in the extreme, and exquisite tropical scenery as a backdrop for classic automobiles, you'll fall in love with the island of Cuba."[1]

Visitors to Cuba put politics aside and find Cuba's people, food, and scenery to be surprisingly enjoyable. The natural landscape alone is breathtaking.

Chapter Five

Because Cuba is a communist country, everyday life there is considerably different than in the US. Cuban children do not have expensive playthings like video game systems or electronic tablets. Instead, they learn how to play various sports and musical instruments. Music is a large part of Cuban culture. Nearly every town has a gathering spot called a *casa de musica* (house of music) where people meet each evening to sing, dance, and listen to music.

Americans who travel to Cuba do not expect to be pampered. "Cubans are passionate and welcoming people, who have a deep-rooted love of music, food, and sports," continued Goldman. "They are resilient and patient as they wait for their great Revolution to give them the many basics of life that are missing on the island. They are incredibly creative and resourceful, making do with very little. The streets in Cuba are surprisingly free of litter, but if you ask where the trash is, Cubans will smile and tell you they have nothing to throw away. They especially enjoy spirited conversation, but they prefer to avoid politics with visiting tourists."[2]

While Cuba doesn't offer much in the way of material luxury, many visitors find its smaller comforts remarkably enjoyable. One of them is traditional Cuban food. John Verlinden is a personal chef who specializes in Cuban cuisine. He is American, but his husband Ozzie Mondejar is Cuban. Mondejar's mother introduced Verlinden to Cuban food in 1985 when she made dinner for him. "I said, oh man, I have to learn how to make this," Verlinden recalled. "She was kind enough to let me work with her and her mother in the kitchen."[3]

Verlinden thinks it's the combination of influences that make Cuban food so appealing. "Spanish and African are the primary influences," he explained, "but also North American. Plus you have the tropical vegetables that make the cuisine so rich. Cuban cuisine is highly seasoned, but it's not spicy. It's *sabor suave*, which means 'soft flavors.'"[4]

Verlinden wrote *To Cook Is to Love*, a book about Cuban history, food, and music based on his mother-in-law's life in her native country. "I've been to Cuba seven times," he added. "We

Cuba

still have family there. We also have a project there. It began as a book project, taking books to libraries. We started taking medical supplies to hospitals and schools for children with disabilities after the horrible hurricane they had a few years back."[5]

Verlinden notes that the Cuban people are generous and welcoming despite their limited resources. "One of the things that's heartbreaking for me is that the average Cuban would have a difficult time getting the ingredients together to make the simplest recipe in the book. You get milk only if you have a baby or an

Traditional Cuban cuisine

Chapter Five

elderly person in the house. Finding spices would be impossible. But if you go to the most humble home, they're going to have Cuban coffee for you and some little treat. And they love to have a good time."[6]

Residents in Havana, Cuba, play dominoes, a common leisure activity.

Ernest Hemingway's Cuban home

An American Icon in Cuba

Ernest Hemingway is among the most famous American writers of all time, and he spent a great deal of his life in Cuba. He purchased a home near the nation's capital of Havana and named it Finca Vigía, which means Lookout Farm. The author wrote seven of his novels—including *The Old Man and the Sea*—while he lived there.

Today, more than 50 years after Hemingway's death, his former home is a museum. Valerie Hemingway was once the author's secretary and later married Hemingway's youngest son, Gregory. In 2007, Valerie returned to Finca Vigía as a writer herself. She wanted to see how much of her late father-in-law's legacy could be found in modern-day Cuba.

She met with the museum's director, Ada Rosa Alfonso Rosales. "As we walked over to the main house after the interview," Valerie recalled, "tourist buses were pulling into the parking lot. The visitors, about 80 percent of them foreigners, peered through the house's windows and French doors—their only option, since a special permit is needed to enter the premises. Even so, I was told this is the most popular museum in Cuba."[7]

While many Cubans link Hemingway to their island, fans from other parts of the world often overlook his time there. Cuban writer Enrique Cirules told Valerie, "For more than 30 years Hemingway had permanent contact with Cuba—in other words, for two-thirds of his creative life. Yet students of his work and life concentrate solely on the European and US years, and the influence of those places on his work. Cuba is never mentioned. I believe it is necessary to delve more deeply into the relationship between Hemingway and his Cuban environment."[8]

Chapter Six
Haiti

One might think of Cuba as a poor country. But it is definitely not the poorest nation in the Caribbean. That unfortunate label goes to Haiti.

Haiti was already one of the poorest places in the world in 2010 when tragedy struck the country. A 7.0-magnitude earthquake occurred on January 12 about 16 miles (25 kilometers) from Port-au-Prince, the nation's capital. Estimates of the death toll range from about 100,000 to more than 300,000, with many more injured. Survivors were left with even less than they had before. To make matters worse, in the aftermath of the quake they had to deal with diseases like cholera.

Some Haitians left in search of better lives elsewhere. For them and for those who remained, preserving customs and traditions has been a way to deal with the devastation—as well as a way to find their identities as Haitians.

Jean Appolon grew up in Port-au-Prince. His family wasn't rich, but they weren't poor either. Appolon was about eight years old when he turned on the television to see Lavinia Williams, a dancer who spent much of her life in Haiti, teaching dance classes at Haiti's National School of the Arts. He was immediately hooked.

But Appolon's father shut the TV off when he saw what his son was watching. He knew it was the poorest Haitians who danced—and followed the voodoo religion that often went along with it. He did not allow either of these things in his household. Girls were allowed to perform other types of dance, but not boys. They were ridiculed if they took part.

Appolon had relatives who practiced voodoo. But he wasn't allowed to see them. His parents had taught him that the sounds of drums were a sign of danger. As a child, Appolon didn't

The 2010 Haitian earthquake devastated towns like Jacmel. Even worse, about 350 people from Jacmel lost their lives.

Chapter Six

understand the role voodoo had played in Haiti's history. When Haiti's slaves revolted against their French masters in 1791, their spiritual beliefs helped unite them. It was the first successful slave revolt in history.

Today many Haitians practice voodoo. Many people think the religion is based in evil and devil worship. But voodoo is not the spooky form of magic that many people assume it is. Rather, it is based in peace and respect. Perhaps part of the problem is the similarly named practice—hoodoo—which includes curses and spells.

Appolon refused to let go of his dreams of becoming a dancer. In 1993, he came to the United States to study at New York's Joffrey Ballet School. Today he works as a professional dancer, teaching at the Boston Ballet School. He sees preserving Haitian culture as part of his job description.

"What dance has really taught me is how rich we are as Haitians and as people of African descent, and the impact of the Afro-Haitian tradition for dance around the world," he explained. "That's something that makes me extremely proud, and I want to be the next generation to represent that."[1]

He also runs a summer dance school in Haiti to help young people connect with their culture. It offers instruction and meals to about 50 students each year. Many of them have no other way of learning about dance and may walk for hours to be part of the four-week program. "The kids really connect to what we are doing," he said. "We're connecting them to their own identity and history. But for kids who have lost family or friends, it became a place where they could transfer some of those feelings and use dance as a way to heal."[2]

Making Haiti a better place for its citizens will take time. But little by little, the nation is moving forward. Susan Semenak of *The Ottawa Citizen* reported, "While the rest of us have been feeling sorry for Haiti, Haiti's been busy getting back on its feet. Though much remains to be done, most of the earthquake debris and tent camps have been cleared away and the government has embarked on an ambitious campaign to bolster tourism."[3]

Haiti

The Jean Appolon Dance Company is seen here performing at the Martin Luther King annual luncheon in Boston. The event celebrates the non-violence teachings of the late civil rights leader.

Chapter Six

Projects in the works include the Champ de Mars in Port-au-Prince. This new plaza has been built to replace the National Palace, ruined in the earthquake. The new facility includes an amphitheater with 5,000 seats, as well as artisan booths and cafes for visitors. Several international hotel chains, such as the Marriott, are also opening on the island. Teachers from a Canadian hotel and restaurant school traveled to the island to train new chefs, waiters, and hotel workers.

Stephanie Villedrouin is Haiti's tourism minister. "We have history, culture, and natural beauty, and we have done colossal work to get ready to welcome tourists back to Haiti," she said. "We don't want charity. We want people to come to Haiti and eat and drink with us, listen to our music and be our guests."[4]

Haiti's capital of Port-au-Prince is slowly recovering from the massive earthquake. The island's leaders hope the Champ de Mars will be the setting of increased tourism and trade in Haiti in the coming years.

Holding on to Her Heritage

Track star Marlena Wesh grew up in the United States. But her parents were born and raised in Haiti before moving to Virginia. When Marlena competed in the 400 meters race in the 2012 Olympics in London, England, she represented Haiti. "I'm the only child that my parents have who considers themselves to be a Haitian-American," she explained. "I actually make an attempt to speak the language and do Haitian things. I embrace the fact that I am a Haitian-American."[5]

Her father pointed out, "Haiti never does anything at the Olympics. So we're very happy that she wanted to run for Haiti. This is a dream come true, really."[6]

Marlena isn't the only outstanding athlete in her family. She was an All-American sprinter at Clemson University, and her brother Darrell earned the same honor at Virginia Tech. Darrell could have competed in the Olympics for Haiti. But as his father explained, "He said he did not want to. I told him it's going to be too hard to make the United States team, but he wanted to run for the USA."[7] Unfortunately, Darrell didn't qualify for the US team.

Marlena's family traveled to London to support her. "I want to try and do my best so I don't let them down," she said on the eve of the Games. "But it hasn't hit me yet about the Olympics. I don't think it will until the opening ceremonies. That's when I'll look around and realize that I'm really here and that I am an Olympian."[8]

She did well enough in her opening heat to advance to the semifinals. But that was as far as she got, finishing eighth in her heat with a time that placed her 19th overall.

Marlena Wesh (left) finishes her heat of the 400 meters in the 2012 Olympics.

Chapter Seven
The Bahamas

Geographically, the Bahamas are not part of the Caribbean. They are located in the Atlantic Ocean, about 50 miles (80 km) southeast of Florida. But they share a great deal of culture with the Caribbean islands, so they are often grouped with them. The archipelago is made up of about 700 small islands with white-sand beaches. The scenery is breathtaking.

The island nation became its own country on July 10, 1973, after being ruled by Great Britain for more than 250 years. The anniversary of the Bahamas' independence is a cause for celebration.

Bernadette Murray is a Bahamian native who lives in Nassau, the nation's capital and largest city. She declared, "I would never live anywhere else. I went to college in North Carolina for four years then went back home. This [independence celebration] is important. . . . It's something that produces jubilation within and immense pride at being a Bahamian. Nothing beats the sense of knowing who you are."[1]

Vacationers pack the beach at Great Stirrup Cay in the Bahamas. The cruise ship *Norwegian Sky* is in the background.

Who are the Bahamians? And what makes them unique? Murray said it's "our food, our people, our culture and our history."[2]

Almost 85 percent of Bahamians are descended from Africans who were brought to the islands as slaves. For this reason there is a large African influence in Bahamian culture. But the islands' centuries under British rule also left their mark on the Bahamas' traditions. For example, one of the most popular festivals is Junkanoo—a celebration held each year on Boxing Day, a popular British holiday on December 26.

The Bahamians credit an African tribal chief named John Canoe for creating Junkanoo. After being taken to the West Indies as a slave, Canoe demanded to be able to celebrate with his people.

Chapter Seven

Today the celebration is marked with a lively parade. Dancers wear colorful costumes and perform to tribal music from drums, horns, whistles, even cowbells. Junkanoo parades are also held in July as part of the independence celebrations.

Festivals are a huge part of Bahamian culture. Art, dance, and music are also a big part of everyday life. The people delight in any excuse to celebrate. The same music heard at Junkanoo can be enjoyed at restaurants and cafes.

Many visitors to the islands enjoy the food. Local seafood, fruits, and vegetables are prepared in a variety of dishes. One of the most popular ingredients in Bahamian food is conch, a shellfish that tastes a bit like an oyster. It can be served many ways. One might enjoy it hot in a chowder or cold as part of a salad. Kids especially like conch fritters, deep-fried chunks of conch.

One resort that offers this tasty treat also offers young people a unique experience: a chance to make Bahamian friends. Kids who visit the Abaco Beach Resort with their parents can take part in its Bahamian Buddies program. It provides young visitors with the chance to get to know local kids through beach and cultural activities. Many Bahamian kids enjoy the same activities other kids do, such as soccer. Young Bahamians may also teach their new friends about fishing and snorkeling. Spending time in the water is a big part of island life.

Bahamian conch salad

The Bahamas

The Junkanoo Festival is filled with dancers in wild costumes.

Chapter Seven

Romeo Farrington is a VIP guide and businessman in Nassau. "We want families who visit to become part of our family," he explained. "Too many visitors come, check into a resort, get off their cruise ship for a few hours to shop and leave without really seeing the Bahamas."[3]

There is much for visitors to experience beyond the resorts and beaches, from swimming with dolphins to exploring the many forts. Located near Nassau, Fort Charlotte is the oldest fortress in the nation. Built in 1788, it includes dungeons and a moat. Another popular attraction is the Queen's Staircase. Its 66 steps carved out of sandstone during the 18th century lead visitors to a spectacular view of Nassau. The Bahamas are also the home of the world's oldest underwater cave system, Lucayan National Park on Grand Bahama Island.

Pierre Vital was born in Haiti. He now lives in the United States. He traveled to the Bahamas to take part in celebrations marking the 40th anniversary of independence. "I haven't been around Bahamian people," he said, "so this is a chance for me to interact with them. I'm interested in Caribbean culture and I go to a lot of cultural events centered on the Caribbean. But one thing I think Caribbean people complain about is that people outside see us as party people and not for the other things we've accomplished."[4]

The Bahamas can definitely boast of accomplishments since the islands' early days of independence, including the creation of several national organizations. The National Insurance Board provides Bahamian citizens with income if they become sick or injured, have a baby, or can no longer work due to age. The Royal Bahamas Defence Force protects the nation's waters. And since the Exchange Control became the Central Bank, the institution has become one of the most respected of its kind in the world.

Dr. Elliston Rahming is the Bahamas ambassador in Washington, DC. He explained, "Our major challenges revolve around economic development. Banking and tourism are our two main industries but we need to further diversify the economy into manufacturing, oil exploration, and light industries. In science, technology and education, we're making our mark, doing well on the world scene."⁵

Paulette Zonicle is the Bahamas' consul-general in Washington. She said, "In addition to agriculture, fisheries and banking, we've also seen our people grow and Bahamians are shoe designers, engineers, doctors, lawyers, designers all spreading around the world. I've grown up with the growth of a new nation. . . . We've elected three prime ministers consecutively with no violence. We change governments smoothly. And 94 percent of Bahamians took part in elections."⁶

Looking upward at the Queen's Staircase. Slaves carved the steps out of solid limestone early in the reign of Queen Victoria, for whom the staircase is named.

Government House, the governor-general's official residence, in Nassau, the Bahamas.

Forty Years and Counting

Governor-General Sir Arthur Foulkes, who took office in 2010, is proud to be a Bahamian. Speaking about the progress his nation has made over the last four decades, he said, "The main thing, as an independent country, is that we have maintained our Parliamentary democracy. That is to our great credit as a lot of former colonies—particularly those in Africa—have had the opposite. We have had four changes of government since 1973 and all went smoothly, without bloodshed!"[7]

Born in 1928 on the Bahamian island of Inagua, Foulkes has been a witness to many changes in the islands during his lifetime. He spent much of his life in the newspaper business, and helped found the *Bahamian Times*.

He added that "We have made other strides as well, such as advances in education, although a lot of improvements could still be made. When I went to Western Senior (now CR Walker), the majority of black Bahamians had to leave school at 14; there was only limited access to Government High School and QC (Queen's College) was segregated. Education has since been expanded and we now have thousands of Bahamians with tertiary degrees—literally thousands! Even some failing schools turn out top-notch students. I firmly believe that it's all about parental interest. In the last few years, we have had five Rhodes scholars from the Bahamas."[8]

Experiencing Caribbean Culture in the United States

Millions of Americans trace their family history to a Caribbean island. As a result, many Caribbean traditions have become part of American culture. These customs are as different as the people themselves. A Caribbean person may be black, white, Latino, East Indian, Chinese, or Arab—or a combination of these races. Likewise, religions differ greatly among Caribbean people. Christians, Muslims, Hindus, and others may trace their origins to the Caribbean.

In 2005, the US House of Representatives voted to designate June as Caribbean-American Heritage Month. Congresswoman Barbara Lee introduced the bill and explained, "People of Caribbean heritage reside in every part of our country. Since before our nation's founding, millions of people have emigrated from the Caribbean to the United States. Throughout US history we have been fortunate to benefit from countless individuals of Caribbean descent who have contributed to American government, politics, business, arts, education, and culture."[1]

Basketball legend Patrick Ewing (born in Jamaica), US Attorney General Eric Holder (whose parents were born in Barbados), and Academy-Award winning actor Sidney Poitier (born in the Bahamas) are just a few of the people with Caribbean origins who have become household names in the United States. Americans also find Caribbean influences in their everyday life, in fields such as fashion, food, and music.

Lee explains, "As we celebrate this month, let us continue to honor the contributions of Caribbean-Americans and all peoples of this rich nation of immigrants, and let us recognize that our diversity will forever be the great blessing and strength of our country."[2]

More than 20 US cities host a wide variety of activities designed to showcase the many facets of Caribbean life during Caribbean-American Heritage Month. These include musical and dance performances, arts and crafts, and booths with Caribbean food.

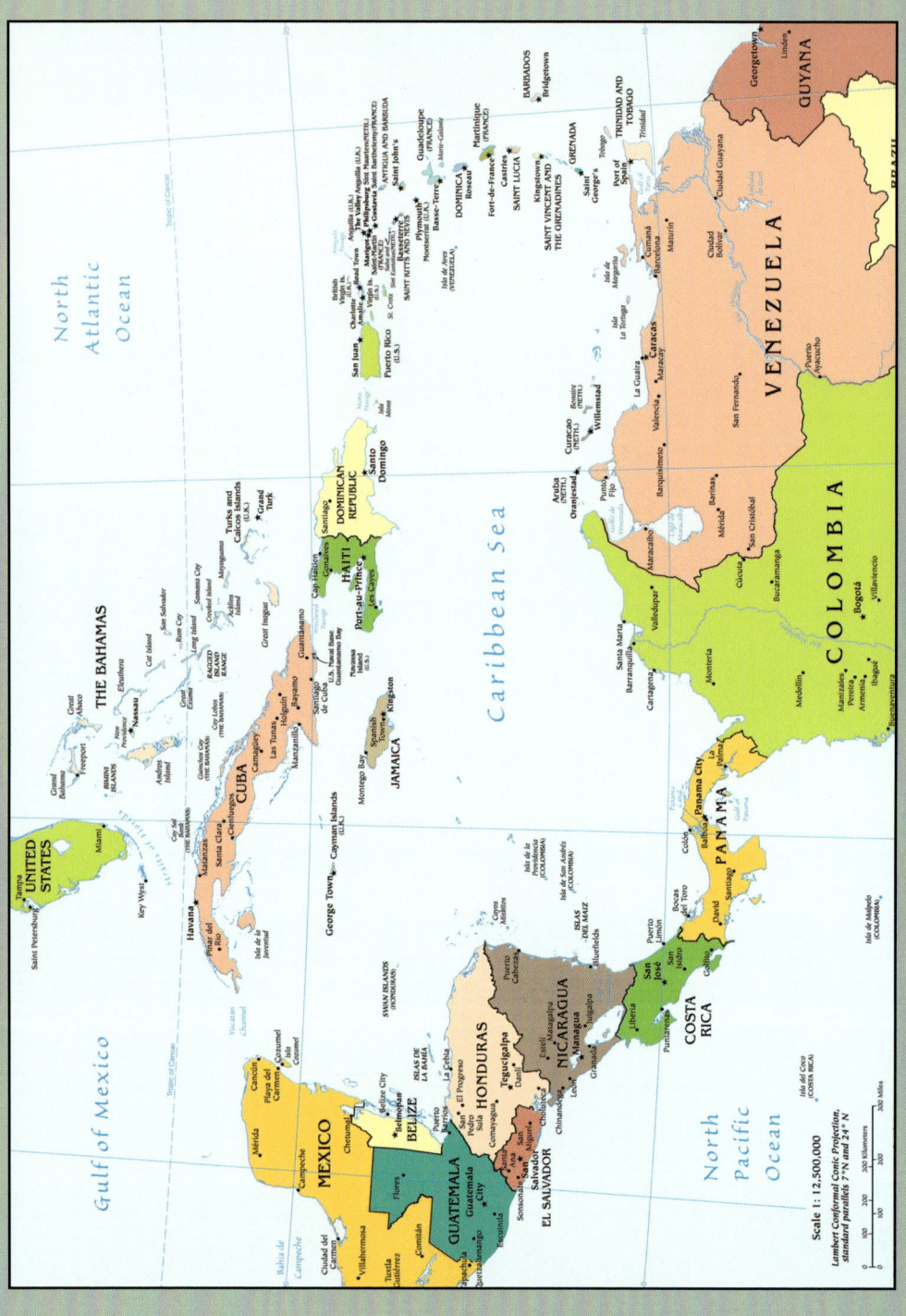

CHAPTER NOTES

Chapter 1: Barbados
1. Anna Tyzack, "Welcome to Barbados: The Caribbean island offers the best of British – with added sunshine." *The Daily Telegraph*, February 20, 2010.
2. John Wilmott, "A vibrant island that's shaped by both history and nature: There's so much to experience in Barbados besides the wonderful beaches and food, which is why is why 2011 is the island's Year of History and Culture, says John Wilmott." *The Daily Telegraph*, November 6, 2010.
3. Mark Eklid, "Mark Eklid's Barbados tour diary." *Derby Evening Telegraph*, March 20, 2013.
4. Lynda Schauf, "The sounds of Barbados." *Redlands Daily Facts*, May 29, 2010.
5. "Sports Tourism Niche Vital for Barbados' Development." Targeted News Service, April 24, 2013.
6. Rihanna, Celebrity Central, People.com http://www.people.com/people/rihanna/biography/0,,20044460,00.html
7. Mark Jeffries, "Young, Rih and single: I NEED A MAN, SAYS LONELY STAR." *The Daily Mirror*, March 2, 2012.

Chapter 2: Jamaica
1. Larry Olmsted, "Island culture is the calling card: Jamaica." *USA Today*, December 10, 2010.
2. "My Jamaica: All eight Star staff members who worked on our Jamaica project in today's Insight section have roots there. They describe their bonds to the Caribbean island." *Toronto Star*, November 4, 2012.
3. Ibid.
4. Ibid.
5. Ibid.
6. Jack Todd, "Jamaican bobsled team drawing lots of attention: Countdown to Calgary." *The Gazette* (Montreal), February 13, 1988.
7. Ibid.

Chapter 3: Trinidad and Tobago
1. Beth Rickers, "From Trinidad to Worthington." *Tribune Business News*, October 25, 2011.
2. Ibid.
3. Ibid.
4. Katie Collins, "Music takes Brush alum Jenny Morgan to Trinidad and Tobago." *The Fort Morgan Times*, February 17, 2012.
5. "Abuja Carnival–Trinidad and Tobago Offers Scholarship to 30 Nigerians." AllAfrica.com, November 25, 2013.
6. T. Cole Rachel, "Nicki Minaj." InterviewMagazine.com http://www.interviewmagazine.com/music/nicki-minaj#
7. Ibid.

Chapter 4: Puerto Rico and the US Virgin Islands
1. Zain Deane, "An interview with Ronald Flores, author of a new book on Puerto Rico." About.com. http://gopuertorico.about.com/od/thelocal/a/An-Interview-With-Ronald-Flores-Author-Of-A-New-Book-On-Puerto-Rico.htm.
2. Ibid.
3. James Estrin, "Puerto Rican Identity, In and Out of Focus." *New York Times*, August 28, 2012. http://lens.blogs.nytimes.com/2012/08/28/an-artists-search-fo-puerto-rican-identity
4. Ibid.

CHAPTER NOTES

5. "Puerto Rico Statehood Resolution Introduced in Senate." *The Huffington Post*, February 12, 2014. http://www.huffingtonpost.com/2014/02/12/puerto-rico-statehood-resolution_n_4777128.html

Chapter 5: Cuba
1. Peggy Goldman, "What to know before you go to Cuba." *The Huffington Post*, May 2, 2013. http://www.huffingtonpost.com/peggy-goldman/what-to-know-before-you-g_b_3195737.html
2. Ibid.
3. Michael Floreak, "Cuban recipes tied to homeland, history, health." *Boston Globe*, April 30, 2014.
4. Ibid.
5. Ibid.
6. Ibid.
7. Valerie Hemingway, "Hemingway's Cuba, Cuba's Hemingway." The Smithsonian.com, August 2007. http://www.smithsonianmag.com/people-places/hemingways-cuba-cubas-hemingway-159858952/?no-ist
8. Ibid.

Chapter 6: Haiti
1. Francie Latour, "Dancing for Haiti: One artist's quest to help preserve the country's culture and promote healing." *Boston Globe*, June 23, 2013.
2. Ibid.
3. Susan Semenak, "Take another look at Haiti: The intrepid Caribbean country is ready for its tourism close-up." *The Ottawa Citizen*, March 22, 2014.
4. Ibid.
5. Larry Rubama, "Running for Haiti." *Virginia-Pilot*, July 15, 2012.
6. Ibid.
7. Ibid.
8. Ibid.

Chapter 7: The Bahamas
1. Barrington M. Salmon, "Bahamas Turns 40." *Washington Informer*, August 8, 2013.
2. Ibid.
3. Eileen Ogintz, "Taking the Kids to the Bahamas: Talk to the locals to get true flavor of Bahamas." *Buffalo News*, July 21, 2013.
4. Salmon, "Bahamas Turns 40."
5. Ibid.
6. Ibid.
7. Adrian Gibson, "What Independence Means to the Bahamas at 40." *Tribune 242*, July 9, 2013. http://www.tribune242.com/news/2013/jul/09/what-independence-means-to-the/
8. Ibid.

Experiencing Caribbean Culture in the United States
1. "Barbara Lee Hails Passage of Caribbean American Heritage Month Resolution." Targeted News Service, June 23, 2010.
2. Ibid.

Photo Credits: All design elements from Thinkstock/Sharon Beck; Cover—pp. 3, 6–7, 8, 9, 16, 17, 28, 29, 30, 31, 34, 36, 37, 39, 41, 42, 48, 49, 50, 54, 55—Thinkstock; pp. 10, 19, 46, 51, 53—cc-by-sa; p. 11—Greg Johnston/DanitaDelimont.com "Danita Delimont Photography"/Newscom; p. 12—Jewel Samad/AFP/Getty Images/Newscom; p. 13—Jonathan Bachman/Eclipse Sportswire/Newscom; pp. 14–15—Dreamstime/Dinogeromella; p. 18—Dreamstime/MaxiSports; pp. 20–21—George Gobet/AFP/Getty Images; p. 22—Dreamstime/Piero Cruciatti; p. 25—Dreamstime/Roger Mcclean; pp. 26–27—Sean Drakes/LatinContent/Getty Images; p. 23—Keystone/Hulton Archive/Getty Images; p. 33—Dreamstime/Roberta Munoz; p. 35—Thais Llorca/EPA/Newscom; p. 40—Dreamstime/Uli Danner; p. 43—U.S. Air Force photo by Master Sgt. Jeremy Lock; p. 45—AP Photo/Lisa Poole; p. 47—Olivier Morin/AFP/GettyImages; p. 56—University of Texas at Austin, Perry-Castañeda Library Map Collection.

FURTHER READING

Books

Hernandez, Romel. *Trinidad and Tobago* (Caribbean Today). Broomall, PA: Mason Crest, 2008.

Sheen, Barbara. *Foods of the Caribbean*. San Diego, CA: KidHaven, 2007.

Spilsbury, Louise. *Living on a Caribbean Island*. Chicago: Heinemann-Raintree, 2007.

Torres, John A. *We Visit Puerto Rico*. Hockessin, DE: Mitchell Lane Publishers, 2010.

Tracy, Kathleen. *We Visit Cuba*. Hockessin, DE: Mitchell Lane Publishers, 2010.

On the Internet

Caribbean Cultural Heritage
http://www.caribbeanculturalheritage.org

Caribbean Traveler
http://www.caribbeantraveler.com/caribbean-culture.html

Lonely Planet, How to Choose a Caribbean Island
http://www.lonelyplanet.com/caribbean/travel-tips-and-articles/77033

Works Consulted

"Barbara Lee Hails Passage of Caribbean American Heritage Month Resolution." Targeted News Service, June 23, 2010.

Caulfield, Keith. "Rihanna Hits 10 Million in U.S. Album Sales." Billboard.com, November 16, 2013
http://www.billboard.com/articles/columns/chart-beat/5793204/rihanna-hits-10-million-in-us-album-sales

Collins, Katie. "Music takes Brush alum Jenny Morgan to Trinidad and Tobago." *The Fort Morgan Times*, February 17, 2012.

Deane, Zane. "An interview with Ronald Flores, author of a new book on Puerto Rico." About.com.
http://gopuertorico.about.com/od/thelocal/a/An-Interview-With-Ronald-Flores-Author-Of-A-New-Book-On-Puerto-Rico.htm

Discovery Channel, Cultural Anthropology
http://curiosity.discovery.com/question/associate-voodoo-evil-devil-worship

Eklid, Mark. "Mark Eklid's Barbados tour diary." *Derby Evening Telegraph*, March 20, 2013.

FURTHER READING

Estrin, James. "Puerto Rican Identity, In and Out of Focus." *New York Times*, August 28, 2012.
http://lens.blogs.nytimes.com/2012/08/28/an-artists-search-fo-puerto-rican-identity/

Floreak, Michael. "Cuban recipes tied to homeland, history, health." *Boston Globe*, April 30, 2014.

Gibson, Adrian. "What Independence Means to the Bahamas at 40." *Tribune 242*, July 9, 2013.
http://www.tribune242.com/news/2013/jul/09/what-independence-means-to-the/

Goldman, Peggy. "What to know before you go to Cuba." *The Huffington Post*, May 2, 2013.
http://www.huffingtonpost.com/peggy-goldman/what-to-know-before-you-g_b_3195737.html

Hemingway, Valerie. "Hemingway's Cuba, Cuba's Hemingway." The Smithsonian.com, August 2007.
http://www.smithsonianmag.com/people-places/hemingways-cuba-cubas-hemingway-159858952/?no-ist

James, Fiona. "Jamaica's in: Enjoy star style, but don't break the bank." *Sunday Mirror*, June 14, 2009.

Jeffries, Mark. "Young, Rih and single: I NEED A MAN, SAYS LONELY STAR." *The Daily Mirror*, March 2, 2012.

Latour, Francie. "Dancing for Haiti: One artist's quest to help preserve the country's culture and promote healing." *Boston Globe*, June 23, 2013.

Marlena Wesh Biography, Clemson Tigers.
http://www.clemsontigers.com/ViewArticle.dbml?DB_OEM_ID=28500&ATCLID=205530011

"My Jamaica: All eight Star staff members who worked on our Jamaica project in today's Insight section have roots there. They describe their bonds to the Caribbean island." *Toronto Star*, November 4, 2012.

Ogintz, Eileen. "Taking the Kids to the Bahamas: Talk to the locals to get true flavor of Bahamas." *Buffalo News*, July 21, 2013.

Olmsted, Larry. "Island culture is the calling card: Jamaica." *USA Today*, December 10, 2010.

"Puerto Rico Statehood Resolution Introduced in Senate." *The Huffington Post*, February 12, 2014.
http://www.huffingtonpost.com/2014/02/12/puerto-rico-statehood-resolution_n_4777128.html

FURTHER READING

"Puerto Rico—History and Heritage." SmithsonianMag.com. http://www.smithsonianmag.com/travel/puerto-rico-history-and-heritage-13990189/

Rachel, T. Cole. "Nicki Minaj." InterviewMagazine.com http://www.interviewmagazine.com/music/nicki-minaj#

Rihanna, Celebrity Central, People.com http://www.people.com/people/rihanna/biography/0,,20044460,00.html

Rickers, Beth. "From Trinidad to Worthington." *Tribune Business News*, October 25, 2011.

Roberts, Peter A. *West Indians & Their Languages*. Cambridge, MA: Cambridge University Press, 2007.

Rubama, Larry. "Running for Haiti." *Virginia-Pilot*, July 15, 2012.

Salmon, Barrington M. "Bahamas Turns 40." *Washington Informer*, August 8, 2013.

Schauf, Lynda. "The sounds of Barbados." *Redlands Daily Facts*, May 29, 2010.

Semenak, Susan. "Take another look at Haiti: The intrepid Caribbean country is ready for its tourism close-up." *The Ottawa Citizen*, March 22, 2014.

"Sports Tourism Niche Vital for Barbados' Development." Targeted News Service, April 24, 2013.

Titus, Mandi. "Tips for the United States Virgin Islands." *USAToday*.com http://traveltips.usatoday.com/tips-united-states-virgin-islands-43432.html

Todd, Jack. "Jamaican bobsled team drawing lots of attention: Countdown to Calgary." *The Gazette* (Montreal), February 13, 1988.

Tyzack, Anna. "Welcome to Barbados: The Caribbean island offers the best of British—with added sunshine." *The Daily Telegraph*, February 20, 2010.

Virgin Islands Now http://www.vinow.com/

Wilmott, John. "A vibrant island that's shaped by both history and nature: There's so much to experience in Barbados besides the wonderful beaches and food, which is why is why 2011 is the island's Year of History and Culture, says John Wilmott." *The Daily Telegraph*, November 6, 2010.

World Music Network, The Music of Jamaica: From Roots to Raggae. http://www.worldmusic.net/guide/music-of-jamaica/

GLOSSARY

archipelago (arh-kuh-PEL-uh-goh)—A group of islands.

cholera (KAHL-er-uh)—Any of several diseases caused by consuming contaminated food or water and marked by severe vomiting and diarrhea.

Commonwealth of Nations (KOM-uhn-welth uhv NAY-shuns)—An international organization consisting of the United Kingdom together with nations that were previously part of the British Empire and dependencies.

emancipation (ih-man-suh-PAY-shuhn)—The freeing of slaves.

indentured (in-DEN-cherd)—A contract in which one person is made to work for another for a certain number of years.

indigenous (in-DIJ-uh-nuhs)—Originating or occurring naturally in a particular region or environment.

jubilation (joo-buh-LAY-shuhn)—An act of rejoicing.

negligible (NEG-lih-juh-buhl)—So small or unimportant as to deserve little or no attention.

prejudice (PREJ-uh-dis)—Unfriendly feelings directed against an individual, a group, or a race.

referendum (ref-uh-REN-duhm)—A vote by the people to approve or disapprove laws or suggested laws.

savory (SAY-vuh-ree)—Pleasing to the taste or smell, often spicy.

tertiary (TUHR-shee-ehr-ee)—The educational level following the completion of a school providing a secondary education.

INDEX

2010 earthquake (Haiti) 42–44, 46
African slaves 8–9, 22, 30–32, 44, 49, 53
Appolon, Jean 42–45
art 9, 32, 37, 43, 46, 50, 55
Bahamas 48–54
Bahamian Buddies 50
Brathwaite, Ryan 12
Boston Ballet School 44
Canoe, John 49
Caribbean-American Heritage Month 55
Castro, Fidel 36
clothing 9, 15, 24, 26, 28, 50
Columbus, Christopher 6–7, 30, 32
Cool Runnings 20
crops
  coffee 30, 40
  cotton 8
  sugar cane 8, 10, 30
  tobacco 8, 30
currency 11
cricket 11–12, 18
Cuba 36–41
dance 19, 38, 42–45, 50–51, 55
economies 24, 52
education 24, 53–55
elections 30, 35, 53
Ewing, Patrick 55
festivals
  Carnival 15, 24–26
  Crop Over Festival 10–11
  Junkanoo 49–51
  Oistins Fish Festival 11
Fleming, Ian 16
food 9–11, 16, 19, 32–33, 38, 49–50, 55
Foulkes, Governor-General Sir Arthur 54
Haiti 42–47
Heinrich, Senator Martin 35
Hemingway, Ernest 41
Holder, Attorney General Eric 55
Husbands, Patrick 12
indentured servants 8, 22
Jamaica 16–20
Jamaican bobsled team 20
Joffrey Ballet School 44
Kennedy, President John F. 16
languages 31, 34, 47
Lee, Congresswoman Barbara 55
Marley, Bob 16, 19
Marley, Ziggy 19
Maynard, Earl 12
Minaj, Nicki 28
Mondejar, Ozzie 38
music
  calypso 26, 34
  reggae 11, 16, 19, 34
  steel pan 34
People-to-People 36
Poitier, Sidney 55
Puerto Rico 30–32, 35
Olympic Games 20, 47
religion 43–44, 55
Rihanna 14–15
Sobers, Garfield 12, 18
Spanish-American War 30
Thompson, Obadele 12
Trinidad 22–28
Tobago 22–26
tourism 26, 44, 46, 52
US Virgin Islands 32–34
Verlinden, John 38–39
voodoo 43–44
Wesh, Darrell 47
Wesh, Marlena 47
Williams, Lavinia 42

About the Author

Tammy Gagne is the author of numerous books for both adults and children, including *We Visit South Africa* and *The Nile River* for Mitchell Lane Publishers. One of her favorite pastimes is visiting schools to speak to children about the writing process. She resides in northern New England with her husband, son, and a menagerie of animals.

Avon Lake Public Library
32649 Electric Blvd.
Avon Lake, Ohio 44012